D0576323

Parents and Caregivers,

Stone Arch Readers are designed to provide enjoyable reading experiences, as well as opportunities to develop vocabulary, literacy skills, and comprehension. Here are a few ways to support your beginning reader:

• Talk with your child about the ideas addressed in the story.

• Discuss each illustration, mentioning the characters, where they are, and what they are doing.

• Read with expression, pointing to each word. You may want to read the whole story through and then revisit parts of the story to ensure that the meanings of words or phrases are understood.

• Talk about why the character did what he or she did and what your child would do in that situation.

• Help your child connect with characters and events in the story.

Remember, reading with your child should be fun, not forced. Each moment spent reading with your child is a priceless investment in his or her literacy life.

Gail Saunders-Smith, Ph.D.

Stone Arch Readers
are published by Stone Arch Books
a Capstone Imprint
1710 Roe Crest Drive
North Mankato, Minnesota 56003
www.capstonepub.com

Library of Congress Cataloging-in-Publication Data
Crow, Melinda Melton.
Rocky and Daisy go home / by Melinda Melton Crow; illustrated by Mike Brownlow.
p. cm. — (Stone Arch readers: My two dogs)
Summary: Rocky and Daisy are shelter dogs longing for a home.
ISBN 978-1-4342-4160-3 (library binding)
ISBN 978-1-4342-6115-1 (paperback)
1. Dogs—Juvenile fiction. 2. Dog adoption—Juvenile fiction. 3. Animal shelters—
Juvenile fiction. [1. Dogs—Fiction. 2. Dog adoption—Fiction. 3. Animal shelters—Fiction.]
I. Brownlow, Michael, ill. II. Title.
PZ7.C88536Rpj 2013
813.6—dc23   2012027141

Reading Consultants:
Gail Saunders-Smith, Ph.D.
Melinda Melton Crow, M.Ed.
Laurie K. Holland, Media Specialist

Designer: Russell Griesmer

Printed in the United States of America in Stevens Point, Wisconsin.
092012
006937WZS13

Go Home

by Melinda Melton Crow
illustrated by Mike Brownlow

STONE ARCH BOOKS
a capstone imprint

ROCKY LIKES:

- Chasing squirrels

- Playing with other dogs

- Chewing things

- Running with me when I ride my bike

DAISY LIKES:

- Playing ball

- Listening to stories

- Resting on the furniture

- Eating yummy treats

Rocky and Daisy were great friends. Rocky was silly and loud. Daisy was sweet and quiet.

They were very different, but
they both loved Owen very
much.

Owen was their owner. He
took them on walks.

He taught them tricks.

He gave them yummy treats.

"We are lucky to have Owen," said Rocky one day.

"We sure are," said Daisy. "Remember the day he adopted us?"

"How could I forget?" asked
Rocky.

Before Owen came along,
Rocky and Daisy lived in an
animal shelter. It was noisy and
crowded in the shelter.

Rocky and Daisy always dreamed of living somewhere else. "I want a real home," said Daisy.

"I want a yard to play in," said Rocky.

Everyday, visitors would come to the shelter and choose dogs to adopt. "Look, Daisy," said Rocky. "Maybe someone will adopt us."

Rocky pressed his nose against
the cage. He wagged his tail and
smiled.

Daisy slid her paws under the cage. She rolled onto her back and grinned.

People always noticed Rocky
and Daisy. But nobody wanted
to adopt them.

Then Owen came to the shelter. Rocky and Daisy noticed Owen right away. "That boy looks fun!" whispered Buddy.

"I bet he would take good care of us," said Daisy. "Let's get his attention."

The other dogs barked, jumped, and howled.

Owen's parents did not like
the noise. So Rocky and Daisy
sat quietly. They smiled and
wagged their tails.

They stood out from the other dogs. Owen noticed them right away.

"Look, Mom," he said. "The sign says their names are Rocky and Daisy. They are friends."

Owen patted the dogs
through the cage. "Maybe we
could get TWO dogs," he said.

Rocky and Daisy grinned.

"I don't know," said Mom.

"Two dogs means twice as much work," said Dad.

"And it means twice as much food," added Mom.

"Please!" begged Owen. "Rocky and Daisy are the nicest dogs here. And it would not be fair to only choose one. They do not want to be apart."

"Well, they are good dogs," said Dad.

Mom knelt down and looked at the dogs. "You are right, Owen. We cannot choose just one."

Rocky and Daisy grinned even bigger.

That day, Rocky and Daisy went home with Owen.

They had a real home. They had a yard to play in. And best of all, they had Owen.

Owen's parents were right. Two dogs meant twice as much food.

It meant twice as much work.

But it meant twice as much fun, too!

THE END

STORY WORDS

adopted   noisy   attention

shelter   whispered

Total Word Count: 418

READ MORE
ROCKY AND DAISY ADVENTURES!